The Race to the Beach!

little bee books
An imprint of Bonnier Publishing Group
853 Broadway, New York, New York 10003
Text and illustration copyright © 2015 by Anna Shuttlewood.
First published in Australia by The Five Mile Press.
This little bee books edition, 2015.
Manufactured in China 1014 HH
First Edition 2 4 6 8 10 9 7 5 3 1
Library of Congress Control Number: 2014921046
ISBN 978-1-4998-0099-9

www.littlebeebooks.com
www.bonnierpublishing.com

The Race to the Beach!

Anna Shuttlewood

little bee books

One sunny day the animals from the zoo decided to go to the beach.

Peacock packed some sunscreen.

Polar Bear put on his sunglasses.

Elephant inflated a beach ball.

Kangaroo found the kite.

Leopard had heard rumors about a train that traveled to the sea.

So the animals made their way to the station, and there it was!

A lovely, shiny, bright red train was waiting on the platform.

Warthog climbed on board.

Anteater hurried to her seat.

Rhino settled back to enjoy the ride.

Soon the zoo animals were on their way.

Before they knew it, the wide blue sea was in front of them.
The happy animals spread out on the warm seaside sand.

Fox looked for lost treasures.

Zebra munched on a juicy watermelon.

Tiger dozed in the summer sun.

And Crocodile built a sandcastle.

The day wore on as the sun rose high.
The zoo animals started to get a little bored.

Then Seal had an idea.

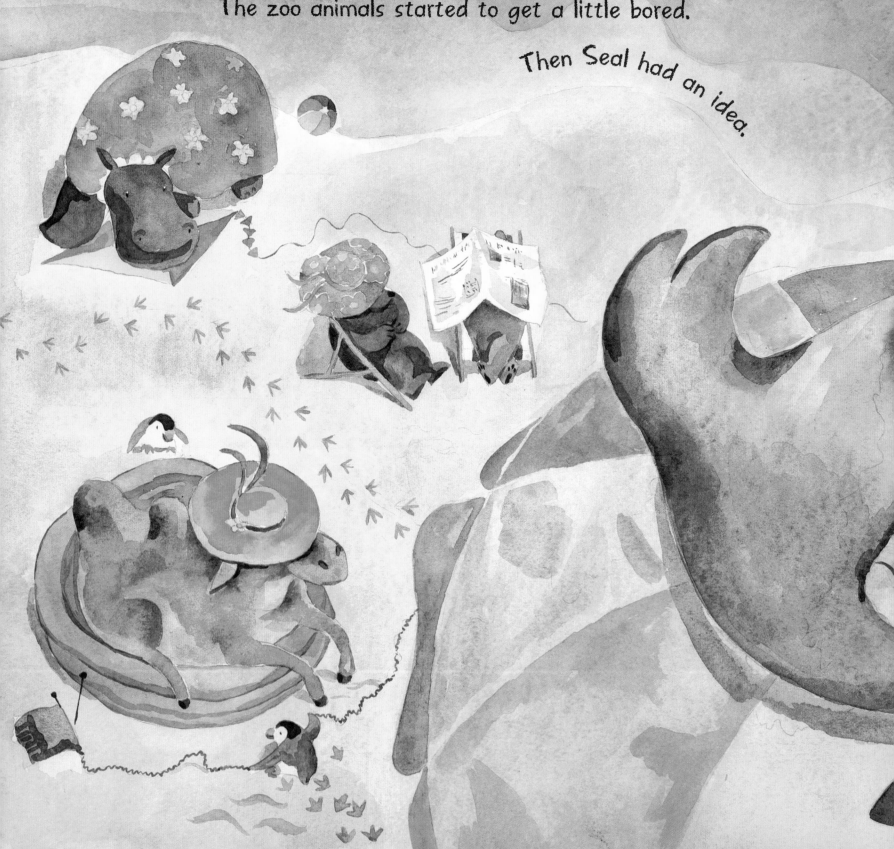

"I know—let's have a race," she said.
"From the seashore to the water.
Whoever can swim out the farthest wins!"

Everyone thought this sounded like a great idea.
And of course, EVERYONE wanted to win.

But Giraffe didn't seem interested in a seaside race.

In fact, Giraffe didn't seem interested in the sea at all.

"Maybe giraffes are afraid of water," said Duck.

"Maybe his spots will wash away!" said Hedgehog.

"Maybe giraffes can't swim!" said Boar.

Giraffe didn't say anything.

The zoo animals prepared for the big competition.

Flamingo stretched.

Yak jumped.

Tortoise practiced his best running leap.

And they all tried out their diving techniques.

Boar landed with a plop!
Lion was ready to make a BIG splash.

"Race time!" called Seal.
The animals stood in a row, ready and waiting for the signal.

The animals dashed toward the water in a
flurry of sand and seaweed.

Polar Bear led the way.

Tiger was a close second. Peacock's feathers
fluttered as she ran.

Boar trailed at the back of the pack.
His little legs just weren't made for beach racing!

Faster and faster the animals swam.
But no one could catch up to Crocodile.

His scaly legs splashed through the water.
His swishy tail moved side to side through the waves.
Crocodile seemed sure to win.

Until...

Giraffe thought he heard a cry.
He looked up, but he couldn't see anything.

He took off his
sunglasses and
stood, stretching his
neck up high.

Then he saw two
scaly arms waving
and splashing
furiously. Giraffe
knew Crocodile was
in trouble.

He ran as fast as he could
into the sea.

Giraffe ran and ran, shells and seaweed splashing behind him.

He ran past Tapir.

He sprinted past Duck.

And he dashed past Antelope.

"HELP!"
shouted Crocodile.

Giraffe reached out with his long, lean neck.
He grabbed Crocodile by the back of his bathing suit
and pulled him out of the water.

Giraffe carried Crocodile from the depths of the sea to the safety of the beach.

The zoo animals unanimously agreed— Giraffe was the winner of the race!

Not only had he rescued Crocodile, but he really
did get the farthest into the sea.

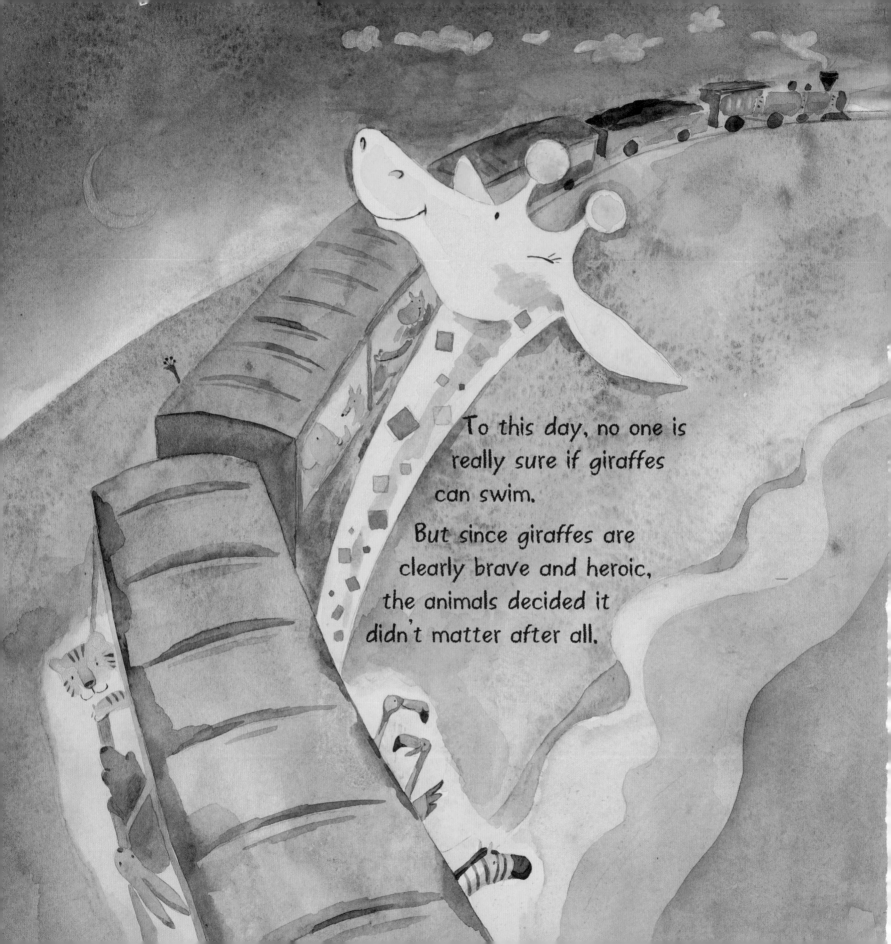

To this day, no one is really sure if giraffes can swim.

But since giraffes are clearly brave and heroic, the animals decided it didn't matter after all.

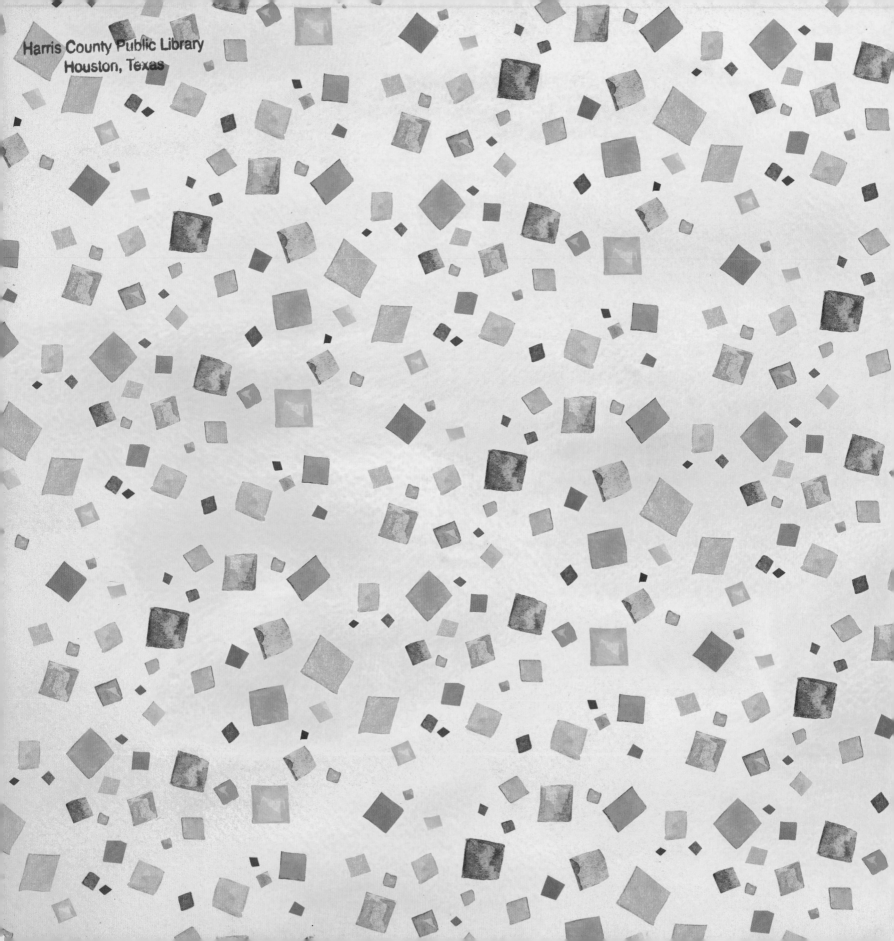